PONY♥DAYS
The Big
Wish

PONY❤DAYS
The Big Wish

Peter Clover

Cover illustration by
Tristan Elwell

SCHOLASTIC INC.

New York   Toronto   London   Auckland   Sydney
Mexico City   New Delhi   Hong Kong   Buenos Aires

ISBN 0-439-80155-9

Copyright © 2000 by Working Partners Ltd.
Created by Working Partners Ltd, London W6 0QT

All rights reserved. Published by Scholastic Inc., 557 Broadway, New York, NY 10012, by arrangement with Working Partners Limited. SCHOLASTIC, APPLE PAPERBACKS, and associated logos are trademarks and/or registered trademarks of Scholastic Inc.

12 11 10 9 8 7 6 5 4   6 7 8 9 10/0

Printed in the U.S.A   40

First Scholastic printing, December 2005

PONY♥DAYS
The Big
Wish

Candlelight
Rescue

Chapter One

"Sheltie! It's Christmas vacation at last!" called Emma.

She opened the paddock gate at the bottom of the yard and rushed over to her little Shetland pony.

Sheltie was busy scratching himself against the hedge at the other side of the paddock. But as soon as he heard Emma's call, he turned his head and trotted over to meet her with a whinny of excitement.

"School finished early today," explained Emma, flinging her arms around Sheltie's neck and giving him a big hug. "And now I've got two whole weeks to spend with you."

Sheltie pushed his soft muzzle into the pocket of Emma's coat. She knew what he was looking for. He was hoping that

there might be a treat inside for him.
Peppermints were his favorite.

"Sorry, Sheltie, no peppermints," said
Emma, laughing. "But I've got a carrot
for you!"

Emma searched in her bag for the carrot
treat and brought out a bundle of bright
cards instead. "Look, Sheltie," she said,
waving them at him. "I've got lots of
Christmas cards from my friends."

The little pony clearly didn't think cards
were as interesting as carrots. He snorted
and nudged at Emma's schoolbag
impatiently.

"Ah! Here's your carrot," said Emma,
pulling it out from the bottom corner of her
bag and feeding it to the little pony. "I'll
get changed out of my school things now,

and then we can ride up the road to celebrate the start of Christmas vacation."

She ran back across the paddock and into the house, bringing a blast of freezing air with her.

"Hello, Emma," said Mom, smiling. There was a delicious smell of baking in the warm kitchen. "Have a little apple pie — but be careful. They're still hot."

"Yum!" said Emma. She gave her little brother, Joshua, a hug and crammed a piece of pie into her mouth.

"Ouch! They really *are* hot!" she cried, waving her hands in front of her mouth. Then Emma ran upstairs to get changed. She pulled on her jeans and a bright yellow sweater and was ready in no time at all.

"I can guess where you're going," said Mom as Emma bounced back into the kitchen.

Emma grinned and grabbed her warm jacket and riding hat.

"It will be getting dark soon," warned Mom, "so don't go far."

"I won't," promised Emma. "Just to the end of the road and back."

This time Sheltie was waiting eagerly at the paddock gate. Emma tacked him up in record time, chatting to him as she worked.

"Mom thinks it might snow, Sheltie. Wouldn't that be great?"

Sheltie snorted loudly as Emma made sure that his girth strap was tight. He seemed to like the frosty weather, too. Once Emma had finished tightening the strap, he pranced happily on all four legs. But as soon as Emma was up in the saddle, he calmed down and walked steadily along the road.

As Emma and Sheltie reached Mr. Crock's house, the door opened and two faces appeared.

"What did I tell you? It's Emma and her Shetland pony," said Mr. Crock.

A little girl with curly brown hair and bright blue eyes peeked out from behind him.

"Hello, Mr. Crock," shouted Emma. "Merry Christmas! Do you have visitors?"

"This is my granddaughter, Rosie," said the old man. He lifted up the little girl, who looked a bit older than Emma's

brother, Joshua. "We heard you trotting down the road. Rosie, come meet Emma and Sheltie."

Sheltie pushed his velvety muzzle toward Rosie. He whickered softly.

"Careful, Sheltie," warned Emma. "Don't frighten Rosie."

But Sheltie was always gentle. Rosie gave a cry of delight and patted Sheltie's mane. "He's beautiful!" she said.

"Rosie's staying here for Christmas," said Mr. Crock. "Her dad has gone to America for an important conference. But he's promised to be back for Christmas Day, hasn't he, Rosie?"

Rosie smiled and nodded, but Emma saw that her eyes were sad. She was obviously missing her dad. Sheltie nosed at her hair, and suddenly, Rosie laughed again. "That tickles!" she said.

Mr. Crock shivered. "It's going to freeze tonight," he said to Emma. "It'll snow in the next day or two, I reckon. I'd better take Rosie inside."

Emma looked at the little girl's sad face and suddenly had an idea. "Would you like to come to my house tomorrow, Rosie?" she asked. "You can ride Sheltie, if you want."

Rosie's eyes lit up. "Can I?" she said. "Oh, Granddad, can I?"

"Yes, of course. I know you'll be safe with Sheltie — he'll look after you," said Mr. Crock. "Thank you, Emma. We'll see you tomorrow, then."

By ten o'clock the next morning, Emma had already fed and groomed Sheltie. She decided to take him out for a short ride before Rosie arrived so that he wouldn't be too frisky for her. Sheltie and Emma enjoyed the ride so much that Emma didn't notice the time. As they trotted back toward the house, she saw two pairs of boots on the doorstep. Mr.

Crock and Rosie must be there already. Emma dismounted and led Sheltie to the back door.

"Let's surprise them!" Emma whispered to her pony.

She tiptoed to the door and Sheltie trod carefully, too, though it was difficult for him to be quiet with his metal shoes. But just as Emma flung open the door, Sheltie decided to give everyone a surprise of his own.

He pushed past Emma, his hooves clattering on the tiled floor, and made straight for the plate of apple pies on the table.

"Oh, no!" cried Mom, and whipped the plate out of Sheltie's reach just in time.

"Sheltie!" shouted Emma. "Get your nose out of there!" She caught hold

12

of his bridle and tried to pull him
back outside.

"Watch your toes, Rosie," said Mr.
Crock, grinning.

Rosie giggled. Emma could see that the
little girl thought this was fun. But she had
to show Sheltie that he shouldn't behave
badly. She tugged the little pony back

outside and tethered him loosely to the paddock fence. Then she raced back into the house.

"Do you still want to ride on such a naughty pony?" Mr. Crock asked Rosie, with a twinkle in his eye.

"Oh, yes!" exclaimed Rosie, her eyes shining.

"He won't be naughty with Rosie, I promise," said Emma. "I'm sorry — I was going to sneak up and surprise you, but Sheltie thought of a better prank!"

"He must have smelled the pies," said Mom, smiling. "Now, let's see if Joshua's helmet will fit you, Rosie."

Joshua's riding helmet fit the little girl perfectly. She went outside and pulled on her boots.

Mr. Crock lifted Rosie onto Sheltie, and
Emma walked the little pony slowly
around the paddock. At first Mr. Crock
held on to Rosie, but soon she was able to
sit in the saddle all by herself. Her eyes
shone with pleasure.

"Good boy, Sheltie," praised Emma.

Sheltie turned his head toward Emma.

His warm brown eyes seemed to be saying, "But I'm always good!"

After Emma said good-bye to Rosie and Mr. Crock, she untacked Sheltie and went back inside. Mom had another visitor! It was Mrs. Price, the principal's wife.

"We're collecting some food and decorations for the senior citizens of Little Applewood," Mrs. Price was explaining. "Some of them don't have much money, and they're finding the winter very hard."

"I've made an extra Christmas pudding," said Mom. "And I can bake another batch of apple pies. But how are we going to deliver the gifts without people thinking we're giving out charity? Some of the senior citizens

16

would hate to think we thought they couldn't cope."

Emma thought hard. There must be some way they could make it fun. Then she remembered how, last Christmas, she and her friends had paraded through the village singing carols.

"Why don't we have a candlelit procession?" she suggested. "I'm sure Sally and my other friends from school would love to be in it. Then we could take everyone a present — just a bag of candy for people who don't really need anything and real food for the people who do."

Mrs. Price looked relieved. "What a wonderful idea, Emma!"

Chapter Two

"How are we going to carry all of this?" asked Sally. "There are only going to be about twenty of us!" She held up a huge basketful of carrots and onions with both hands.

Emma looked at her best friend in dismay. "You're right. And the little children will be able to carry even less. Just look at all those potatoes!"

The village hall was full of goodies.

There were pies, Christmas puddings, and fresh vegetables and fruit. There was holly, mistletoe, and paper decorations, too.

Lots of Emma's school friends had agreed to take part in the procession. It was planned for the next evening, and they were all busy packing baskets full of gifts in the village hall. But now they were faced with an even bigger problem.

"We've got to carry lanterns as well," Dylan pointed out.

"So that leaves just one hand to carry a basket," said Robert.

Alice, Josie, and Tracy tested how heavy the baskets were and shook their heads. *They* could just manage to carry them, but their little brothers and sisters would never be able to.

"We'll have to keep coming back for more, I suppose." Mrs. Price sighed. "Perhaps we should forget about the lanterns."

Emma was disappointed. The whole point of a candlelit procession was to have candles. And if they had to keep coming back to the village hall, it wouldn't be much of a procession, either.

"There must be a way," said Emma to Sally.

Emma racked her brains all evening before she went to bed. When she woke up the next morning, her head was still buzzing with the problem.

I'll take Sheltie for a ride, Emma said to herself. *Maybe that will help me think*.

While Emma put on Sheltie's tack, she

told him all about the problem. When he was ready, Emma led him through the paddock gate and past the garage doors.

Suddenly, Sheltie stopped. He tossed his mane and blew a loud raspberry.

He stamped his feet and pushed his head against the garage doors. They made a loud clanking noise. Emma tugged at the pony's reins and tried to pull him away, but Sheltie simply tugged back and pawed at the doors with his hooves.

"Don't do that, Sheltie!" said Emma. "Mom and Dad will be mad if you scrape all the paint off! What's the matter?"

Emma pulled open the door and poked her nose inside. Sheltie poked his nose inside, too, and whinnied loudly. There stood Sheltie's little fish cart.

"Of course!" she said. "We can carry the baskets around in your cart! Brilliant! Is that what you were trying to tell me, boy?"

Sheltie blew hard down his nose and Emma gave him a hug. "You're such a smart pony, aren't you?"

Once Sheltie was out of the garage, Emma shut the doors again, tethered her pony to the fence, and ran inside to tell Mom.

"It's certainly big enough to take all the food baskets around the village," said Mom.

"And everybody will have their hands free to carry their lanterns," said Emma. "The candlelit procession will happen after all!"

"That cart will need a good cleaning, though," said Mom. "Maybe Rosie would like to help. She needs cheering up because she's missing her dad."

Emma took Sheltie for a short ride and visited Rosie on her way back home.

Rosie wanted Sheltie to help wash the cart, too, so the three of them crowded into the garage. Emma got a big pail of soapy water and two sponges — one for her and one for Rosie.

Sheltie watched the two girls curiously. He bent his head to investigate.

"Don't drink that, Sheltie!" cried Emma.

But before she could move the pail away from him, the Shetland pony blew into the water. Lots of little bubbles frothed up and clung to his mane and ears.

Rosie giggled. "He looks funny! He's like Santa Claus, with a big white beard!"

Sheltie sneezed, and bubbles floated all over the garage. Rosie laughed again, and by the time Mr. Crock came to pick her up she was very cheerful. The fish cart looked as good as new, and Emma and Rosie had even decorated it with some trailing ivy.

As Emma was saying good-bye to Rosie, she had another idea. "Why don't you come with us, Rosie?"

Rosie shook her head and looked at the floor.

"There will be a lot of strange people," explained Mr. Crock. "She gets a little shy."

Emma thought hard, then said, "Will you come if you can ride Sheltie in the procession?"

Rosie's eyes sparkled. She beamed and said, "Ride Sheltie? Oh, yes, *please*!"

Chapter Three

When everybody met at the village hall that evening, it was just beginning to get dark.

Emma and her friends were putting the finishing touches on the baskets. Josie, Tracy, and Alice put on their thick winter gloves and tied prickly holly to the sides. Mrs. Price helped Rosie tie a ribbon on top. As soon as each basket was ready, Emma and Sally placed it in the decorated cart.

Suddenly, there was a shriek from Rosie. "Sheltie! Sheltie!"

Emma spun around.

The little pony was trotting through the hall toward them. Somehow he had managed to pull his tether rope loose from the ring outside the hall and push his way inside. Sheltie had been good all day, but Emma knew how much he hated to be left outside when there were exciting things happening. Before Emma could stop him, he had helped himself to a large carrot.

"Oh, Sheltie, how did you get free?" cried Emma. She and Sally quickly led him away from the delicious vegetables and took him back outside.

Dylan and Robert laughed so much that

they nearly fell into the cart full of baskets. Mrs. Price was annoyed with them.

"If you can't behave, you two, go outside and make sure that Sheltie doesn't sneak back in," she said.

At last everything was ready, and Sheltie was allowed to take his position in between the shafts of the loaded cart. He skittered a

bit on the polished floor of the hall and
gave a loud, wet blow right down Rosie's
neck. The little girl giggled. "That was
yucky, Sheltie!"

"Make sure you behave once we're out
on the street," warned Emma in her
sternest voice.

Sheltie looked at her innocently through
his long forelock, as if to say, "Don't I
always behave?"

By now it was really dark, but the
members of the procession had their
twinkling lanterns to guide them through
the village. Mrs. Price led the way. Rosie
sat proudly on Sheltie's back, with Emma
and Sally walking on each side of the little
pony. Mom followed at the back of the
procession to make sure that everyone
was safe.

Mrs. Price and Mom knew Little Applewood very well. Whenever they reached a house where a senior citizen lived, Emma would bring Sheltie to a halt. Then she and her friends would deliver a basket of goodies.

It was easy to give out the little bags of candy, too. Nearly all of the villagers came out of their homes to watch the procession, anyway, so Robert and Dylan just handed them each a present.

"Are you having a nice vacation with your granddad, Rosie?" asked Mrs. Marsh as the procession stopped at her house.

"Yes, but my daddy will be here for Christmas, too," said Rosie bravely.

"I know, dear," said Mrs. Marsh, peering eagerly into her gift basket.

Suddenly, Rosie cried out in alarm. Emma saw what her mischievous pony was up to. Sheltie was trying to turn his plump little body in the shafts. He had pushed his shaggy head around as far as it would go and was trying to reach an apple from one of the baskets in the cart.

"Don't worry, Sheltie, I've saved you an apple for later!" said Emma kindly as she pulled at his reins.

Sally grinned across at her, and Emma couldn't help giggling. Sheltie was naughty, but so funny at the same time. Emma tried to look stern. "Now then, boy, you must behave." She clicked her tongue, and they all moved off to the next group of houses.

Everyone cheered as they watched the procession go by with its gleaming lanterns. The villagers were all thrilled with their gifts.

Finally, they came to the last house in the village. This was set apart from most of the other houses. It looked very dark and lonely.

"All the lights are off," said Emma with a frown. "Do you think Mr. Bates has gone away for Christmas?"

"Let's knock," said Dylan. He and

Robert raced ahead and pounded at the door.

"No answer," they called as they came back. "Maybe he's asleep."

"Let's just go make sure," said Mom. "It won't do any harm."

"Walk on, Sheltie," said Emma. "This is the last house."

Sheltie blew a snort and turned his big shaggy head toward the nearly empty cart. His eyes twinkled brightly in the candlelight. The little pony tossed back his hairy head so that his bridle jingled, then gave a very loud whinny.

"If Mr. Bates was asleep, he won't be now," said Emma, giggling as she lifted the last basket down from the cart.

Sheltie pulled up right beside the high

windows of the house. Rosie peeked in
from Sheltie's back.

"Oh, I can see a light!" shouted Rosie.
"It's flickering — he's got a candle
like ours."

"A candle?" said Mom quickly. "Can
you move Sheltie out of the way a

moment, please, Emma, and I'll take
a look."

She stood on tiptoe, peered through the
window, and gasped. "You're right, Rosie.
There is just a candle," she said. "Poor Mr.
Bates is sitting wrapped in blankets. He
looks very cold and lonely. I wonder
what's the matter."

Chapter Four

"Mr. Bates! Mr. Bates!" called Emma and Sally together. Everyone joined in and Sheltie added to the noise with his loudest whinny! Rosie banged on the window from Sheltie's back.

"Hush!" said Mrs. Price. "We won't be able to hear him." She pressed her ear to the door.

Then they all heard his voice. "I can't open the door," he said weakly. "I'm too

cold to move and that'll let all the cold
air in!"

"Oh, dear!" said Emma anxiously. "What
can we do to help?"

"I'll see if I can get Officer Green on my
cell phone," said Mom. "We have to get in
somehow."

"Don't stand still, everyone," called Mrs.
Price. "It's too cold. Have a race to the field
gate and back."

"Me, too!" said Rosie.

Mom lifted Rosie down and they all
stuck their lanterns into Mr. Bates's tidy
front yard.

"One, two, three, GO!" shouted Mrs.
Price.

Everyone raced off except Emma,
who stayed to look after Sheltie and
the cart. Mom switched on her phone

and began to dial the policeman's number.

"Where are you going now, Sheltie?" asked Emma as her pony disappeared around the side of the house. She quickly followed him.

Now that he wasn't responsible for Rosie, Sheltie seemed to be very interested in the house. He knocked his little fish cart into the stone wall as he nudged against a small window on the side wall. An icy wind whipped around the corner and banged on the window in its frame.

"The latch must be broken!" said Emma. "No wonder poor Mr. Bates is so cold. It must be really drafty in there."

Sheltie snorted into Emma's neck and pushed her gently toward the wall. One of the cart wheels banged against the house again.

"Be careful, Sheltie!" cried Emma. "We don't want to break your cart."

But the Shetland pony wouldn't stop nudging at Emma. Finally, he lifted his shaggy head as if to point to the window and blew a loud raspberry.

"Wait a minute . . ." said Emma slowly. "I think I could fit through that window. I wonder what's on the other side. Stand still, boy, while I get up and look."

She hauled herself up onto Sheltie's back, and the little pony stood as steady as a rock beneath her. Emma pushed at the window, and it opened a little way. There was just enough space for her to wriggle through.

Mom had finished her call to Officer

Green and came to see what Emma was trying to do. "Emma, be careful!" she said. "You shouldn't try climbing through there!"

"It's all right, Mom," said Emma. "There's a sofa right underneath. I'll be safe." Then she called through the window to Mr. Bates. "I'm going to come in and help you, Mr. Bates! Don't be frightened."

Sheltie stood very still while Emma grabbed hold of the window frame and squeezed herself through headfirst.

Then she carefully wriggled down toward the comfy sofa.

"Easy-peasy!" she said, and with a final wriggle she tumbled in a heap onto the sofa cushions. Sheltie gave a high, excited whinny from outside.

"It's all right, Mr. Bates," said Emma, rushing over to where he was sitting wrapped in blankets.

Mr. Bates managed a smile. "I've run out of money for the electricity," he mumbled. "I've run out of wood, too — and it's so cold, I just couldn't bear to go outside to get some more. I didn't want to let you in, either, because of the cold air. I — I thought I'd never get warm again if I did that."

"We've come to help," said Emma. "We've got a special Christmas food basket

for you, and we can bring in some logs for
your fire. I won't open the door very far,"
promised Emma, "but I'm going to let
Mom in."

She unbolted the front door and Mom
squeezed through, trying not to let in too
much cold air.

Emma quickly explained to Mom that there were no lights or heat. By then all the other children had come back from their race and were waiting in the front yard.

"Why haven't you phoned your daughter, Mr. Bates?" asked Mom. "She lives nearby, doesn't she? I'm sure she'd have come and helped."

"She's got the flu, and the children are sick, too," said Mr. Bates stubbornly. "I don't want to be a nuisance."

"She won't think you're a nuisance," said Mom. "Nobody should be on their own at this time of year. Let me call her, and you can have a chat. But first I'm going to phone Officer Green and tell him you're all right."

Emma opened the door a little way, and everyone crowded in. Mrs. Price brought in the last of the goodies. It was so crowded inside Mr. Bates's house that it began to feel warm immediately. Emma ran back outside to tether Sheltie to a tree. Tracy and Sally brought in armfuls of logs, and Mom soon coaxed the fire to burn brightly.

Then Mom talked to Mr. Bates's daughter on the phone. She was horrified that her father had said nothing about his problems. She said she would come over right away and take Mr. Bates home for Christmas.

"Your grandchildren are feeling better now," Mom explained to Mr. Bates with a smile. "Your daughter will be here in an hour."

Mr. Bates grinned with relief.

"An hour? Great!" shouted Robert. "We can have a party here while we're waiting!"

The fire was roaring up the chimney now, and there were pies, cakes, and oranges to eat. Sally and Tracy hung paper decorations on the walls, while Dylan and Robert tried to tuck holly behind the pictures without pricking themselves. Mom called everyone's parents on her cell phone to explain why they were going to be home a little late.

"I didn't expect a party." Mr. Bates laughed, his mouth full of pie.

"It's all thanks to Sheltie," said Emma. "He found the open window."

"I wish there was room for him in here," said Rosie sadly.

Sheltie obviously agreed. He had managed to pull his tether rope free and was kicking rather loudly at the front door! Emma opened it just a little way.

Everybody burst out laughing when Sheltie's furry head peered into the room. His eyes twinkled as he looked around at

all his friends. Then he blew a very loud raspberry.

"Well, this *is* a different Christmas!" said Mr. Bates, laughing. "I've never had a Shetland pony do that before!"

A Christmas
Star

Chapter One

"Look at Sheltie!" said Rosie, laughing. "He's so funny!"

"Oh, no!" cried Emma. She rushed over to the other side of the village hall just before Sheltie knocked some scenery over. "Sheltie, you're messing everything up!" she said.

After all the excitement of the candlelit procession, the younger children of Little Applewood had to continue rehearsing for the nativity play. This was going to be held in the village hall on Christmas Eve. Mrs. Price, who was organizing the play, had asked some of the older children to help with the costumes and scenery, and Sally and Emma had brought Rosie along with them. The little girl had insisted that Sheltie come inside, too.

"Stay here, Sheltie, where I can keep an eye on you," said Emma. She led the pony closer to where she and Sally were working on some paper crowns for the Three Kings.

Sheltie seemed very interested in the gold and silver paper lying on the floor. He grabbed at a length with his strong teeth and flicked it over his shaggy head. He pulled at another length and managed to

wind it around his thick neck. Then he
pawed at a heap of clothes, and soon his
legs were all tangled up in them! Sheltie
looked pretty silly with paper draped
over him and his legs tangled up in a
shepherd costume!

"Sorry, Rosie. We'll have to take him

outside," said Emma. "He's just too naughty to be in here." She could see that Rosie was upset. When Sheltie was around, the little girl seemed to forget about her dad not being there.

Emma took Sheltie outside and tethered him to the railings by the door. It was then that she had an idea.

"Maybe Rosie could be in the play," she suggested to Sally. "Mrs. Price," she called, "can Rosie be a shepherd?"

"What a good idea," said Mrs. Price. "I've got an extra costume."

But Rosie didn't seem sure about being a shepherd, even when Emma said that her little brother, Joshua, was going to be a shepherd, too.

"Mudlark!" said Joshua, making a funny *hee-haw* noise.

"Oh, yeah! Joshua just reminded me," said Emma. "Marjorie Wallace, Mudlark's owner, said we could borrow him because we need a donkey in the play. In fact, Mudlark will be coming to the dress rehearsal tomorrow," Emma went on. "So, Rosie, would you like to be a shepherd now?"

Rosie looked very excited. She loved animals. "Yes, please!" she said.

It was Christmas Eve. Emma and Sheltie picked up Rosie on their way to the morning dress rehearsal.

But Rosie had changed her mind about being a shepherd. "I want to stay home in case Daddy comes," she said.

"Her dad's been delayed because of the bad weather," explained Mr. Crock. Then he turned to Rosie. "You don't want to miss being in the play," he said to the little girl. "Everyone's coming to watch you tonight."

Sheltie threw back his shaggy head and blew a loud raspberry. Rosie giggled.

"Sheltie wants you to come," said

Emma. "And remember, Mudlark will be there, too."

Rosie's eyes gleamed as she remembered Mudlark. "OK, I'll come," she said. "But can I give Sheltie a carrot first?"

Mr. Crock's eyes twinkled. "Keep him away from my vegetables," he said gruffly to Emma as he went inside to get a carrot for the pony. Mr. Crock was very proud of his garden. Even in the freezing cold, there were Brussels sprouts growing in his neat vegetable beds.

Sheltie took the carrot gently between his lips and blew softly into Rosie's outstretched palm. His dark eyes twinkled through the mass of hair over his face.

Emma helped Rosie put on Joshua's riding hat. Then Mr. Crock lifted the little girl onto Sheltie's back and they were off.

"Walk on gently, Sheltie," said Emma.

Sheltie stepped out proudly, as if Rosie were a little princess on his back. He didn't seem to need Emma to tell him what to do!

"Can Sheltie come in?" asked Rosie when they reached the hall. She slid off his back by herself, with Emma watching to make sure she didn't stumble when she reached the ground. Sheltie turned to Emma and looked at her with his big brown eyes.

"No, Sheltie, there are too many things to knock over inside," said Emma firmly. "Would you like to help me take his saddle off and tether him to the railings,

Rosie?" She showed Rosie the special knot that she used to loosely tether the pony.

Once they were back inside, Rosie soon forgot about Sheltie. There was so much to do.

Emma and Sally had to make sure that all the actors were wearing the right costumes and standing in the right place. Then they took their places on either side of the stage. It was their job to draw the curtains at the beginning and end of each scene. They were only missing one actor now . . . Mudlark.

"Marjorie promised she'd be here in time," said Mrs. Price. "We're half an hour late already. I suppose we'll just have to start without the donkey."

Emma was worried. It wasn't like

Marjorie to be late. Emma hoped that there was nothing wrong.

Suddenly, the doors of the hall burst open. It was Marjorie at last. But where was Mudlark? There hadn't even been a

whinny from outside. Surely Sheltie would have greeted his old friend?

Mrs. Price stopped the rehearsal and hurried over.

"I'm so sorry, everyone," said Marjorie with a gasp. She was panting, as if she had been running. "Mudlark's gone lame. I only found out this morning, so it was too late to call you, Mrs. Price. It's not serious, but I'm afraid you won't have a donkey for Mary to ride in the play!"

Chapter Two

Everyone crowded around as Marjorie explained about Mudlark.

"He was fine yesterday," she said. "But some time early this morning he must have slipped on an icy patch outside his shed and twisted his foreleg."

Poor Mudlark! thought Emma.

Marjorie told them that the donkey's knee was badly swollen, and the vet had said Mudlark would be out of action for the next few days. They couldn't borrow Sophie, Marjorie's other donkey, either. Her brother, Todd, had taken Sophie to visit friends for the day and wouldn't be back until late.

"Never mind," said Mrs. Price briskly to the children. "Mudlark's going to be all right, that's the main thing. And we don't really need a donkey. Mary will just have to walk."

"It won't be the same, Mrs. Price!" said Wayne, who was playing Joseph. They had all been looking forward to having a donkey in their play.

After Emma said good-bye to Marjorie, she turned to find Rosie by her side.

"Go on, Rosie," she said gently. "You've got to go and be a shepherd now."

"I wish Mudlark was here." Rosie sighed

and walked slowly back to join the rest of the shepherds. Just then, there was a loud whinny from outside.

"Sheltie!" exclaimed Emma, and rushed outside.

Sheltie was shaking his head backward and forward and yanking at his tether rope. When he saw Emma, he gave another great whinny.

"Sheltie, what's the matter? Has someone been teasing you?" cried Emma. She looked up and down the street, but there was no one around.

Sheltie neighed and tossed his shaggy mane so that it flew around his head like a lion's mane. Then he pawed at the ground and pulled hard on his tether rope again.

"Are you just making a fuss because you can't come inside?" said Emma. She put her arms around his neck and hugged him. "Calm down, boy. The rehearsal won't take long now."

But Sheltie didn't seem to want to calm down. He kept on shaking his head and pulling at his tether rope as if he was trying to get in through the doors of the hall.

"You know you can't go in there," said Emma firmly. "You'll distract Mudlark from his job. . . ."

And then she suddenly remembered. Of course! Mudlark wasn't in the hall, and there was no donkey for the Christmas play. Maybe Sheltie could take Mudlark's place. . . . After all, he had drawn Cinderella's coach in their school play last year. He was a good actor, but would he behave himself? It was worth a try.

"Come on, then, boy," she whispered. "Let's go tell everyone that Mary can ride to the stable on a Shetland pony instead of on a donkey!"

Emma led the little pony into the hall. All the actors clapped and cheered when Emma suggested that Sheltie could take Mudlark's place. But Mrs. Price wasn't so sure.

"I seem to remember that Sheltie doesn't always behave himself," she said uncertainly. "We don't want him eating the scenery."

But everyone else protested.

"He'll be a wonderful donkey, Mrs. Price," said Wayne.

"I'm sure he'll be good," said Rosie anxiously. She really wanted Sheltie to be onstage with her.

"All right, then," said Mrs. Price at last. "But you have to look after him, Emma.

Put his saddle back on and make sure he behaves. The first time he nibbles a costume, he's out!"

Sheltie looked at Mrs. Price and slowly blinked his dark, twinkly eyes. He walked up to the stage, as good as gold, and climbed onto the low platform. Then he turned around and shook his mane gently as if to say, "There! Didn't I do that well?"

Mrs. Price lifted the little girl playing Mary onto Sheltie's back. The pony stood still as a rock for her.

Rosie tugged at Emma's hand. "Can I lead him?" she whispered.

"I don't think a shepherd would lead a donkey," said Emma, worried.

But Mrs. Price had heard Rosie, too. "As you've been learning how to look after Sheltie, Rosie," she said, "how would you like to be the innkeeper's daughter instead of a shepherd? Then you can show Mary's donkey where the stable is."

Rosie went pink and nodded. Sheltie blew gently down his nose and nodded his shaggy head, too.

Emma showed Rosie how to hold on to Sheltie's reins and lead him. The Shetland pony behaved perfectly. He walked slowly across the stage with Mary on his back and stopped right by the manger. Sheltie waited until Emma and Sally drew the curtains across to end the scene, then stretched out his neck toward the sweet hay.

"No, Sheltie," said Rosie in a stern voice. She sounded just like Emma

69

when she was trying to be strict with
Sheltie. This made Emma giggle.
Rosie was doing a very good job with
the little pony.

The next scene was set after the baby was born. Once the children had sung a carol, Mary was supposed to put the baby down into the manger. But Mary couldn't quite reach the manger from her chair. Mrs. Price rushed up onto the stage to push the manger forward.

As the teacher was bending over the crib, Sheltie turned his head and gave her bottom a sly nudge. The children couldn't help laughing.

"Sheltie! You naughty pony!" said Mrs. Price.

Emma scolded Sheltie.

"If you don't behave, I'll have to take you home," she told him severely.

The Shetland pony hung his head as if he was sorry. Then he lifted it up and blew a long, loud raspberry that made everyone laugh again.

When Emma saw the mischievous glint in his eye, she knew there could be more trouble to come.

Chapter Three

"There'll never be time to do everything!"
cried Emma once she was back at the house
that afternoon. "I want to take Sheltie for
a ride, even if it's a short one. If he doesn't
have some exercise, he'll run around and
do something naughty during the play.
Then I've got to have dinner, then clean
Sheltie's hooves —"

"And after all that, you've got to

hang up your stocking!" interrupted Dad with a smile.

"Oh, yeah!" said Emma, clapping her hand to her head. "There's so much to do, I forgot it's Christmas Day tomorrow!"

"Calm down, Emma," said Mom. "You can have a quick sandwich now. The play won't end very late, so we can eat a real dinner when we come back. And I'm afraid you really can't go for a ride. The weather forecast says that heavy snow is coming. It's already started — look."

Emma looked out the window. Snowflakes were swirling around over Sheltie's paddock. "Wow! We're going to have a white Christmas after all!" she said happily.

She did have time to give her little pony

a brush-down. He still had pieces of gold
and silver paper stuck in his mane from the
dress rehearsal. Emma brushed hard, but
there was no way Sheltie could ever look
really tidy.

"It's good you're supposed to be a
donkey and not a show pony, Sheltie," she
told him. She leaned against his fat little

tummy so that she could lift his leg and work at the feathery tufts above one of his hooves.

Sheltie stamped his hoof against the ground when she let it down. Then he lifted the next leg for her to brush with no trouble at all.

"Good boy, Sheltie. I hope you behave as well as this in the play," said Emma.

Sheltie looked at her with his melting brown eyes. Emma flung her arms around his neck, burying her face in his shaggy mane. "I'm sorry, Sheltie. I know you're going to be the best actor in the play tonight!"

The village hall was packed. Everybody in Little Applewood had come to see the Christmas play. Emma saw lots of her friends. There was Mrs. Pinkerton from the corner shop, Charlie from the garage, and Mr. Samson from the candy shop. Mr. Crock sat in the front row with Emma's mom and dad and Sally's parents. When Rosie led Sheltie onto the stage with Mary on his back, Mr. Crock clapped very loudly. But Rosie didn't look at him once. She kept looking straight ahead, just like Emma had told her.

"Whoa, Sheltie," she said, and Sheltie stopped right away. After Mrs. Price had lifted Mary down from the little pony, Rosie led Sheltie to stand behind the manger.

Emma kept an eye on Sheltie from where she was standing by the curtain — just in case. Sheltie looked back at her with a twinkle in his eye. He stood as still as a statue.

At the end of the performance, all the actors bowed, and everybody clapped and cheered. Sheltie stood patiently behind the actors, waiting for everybody to finish bowing.

It was a long time for a little pony to stand still. And nobody had asked Sheltie to come forward to take a bow. Emma was just wondering whether she should go and bring him forward when suddenly, the Shetland pony pushed his way gently through the children. He stopped just behind the manger.

"Isn't he clever!" cried someone in the audience as Sheltie bent his head in a bow.

But Emma could see what Sheltie was
really trying to do. She hissed to Sally,
"Close the curtains! Quick!"

Sally looked at Sheltie and quickly drew
her curtain. But she couldn't help laughing.
The pony wasn't bowing at all. His head
was bent into the manger, and he was

stealing a mouthful of hay from underneath the doll baby!

While all the children and the audience ate their feast of pies and cake, Emma took off Sheltie's saddle and gave Rosie a peppermint to palm to him as a special reward.

"He was very good *nearly* all the time," said Emma. She gave the little pony a big hug.

Sheltie nuzzled Rosie as if to say that they were a great team.

Gradually, the villagers began to put on their coats, scarves, and hats. Mrs. Price, Emma, and Sally packed the costumes in a big box to take back to school after Christmas. It was time for everyone to go home and hang up their stockings.

Emma's dad went to open the hall doors. But when he tried to push them open, they wouldn't budge!

"Has somebody locked the door?" he asked.

He pushed again and the doors opened just a little way. A huge blast of icy wind came into the hall. Through the crack, Emma and Dad could see a great white wall of snow!

Chapter Four

"Wow!" Emma gasped. The wall of snow was almost as high as Sheltie.

"What are we going to do?" said Dad anxiously. "It looks as though the wind's blown all the snow against the hall doors."

"A snowdrift!" said Mr. Crock, peering over Dad's shoulder.

"We'll soon shove our way out," said

Charlie confidently from the garage. "We just need a few strong people."

Sally's dad came forward, and so did several other people.

"Push, everyone," ordered Charlie. "All together now — one, two, *three*!"

Mr. Samson, Charlie, Mr. Jones, Dad, and the others all shoved hard. But outside

the doors the snow had piled up so thickly that pushing just seemed to pack it tighter.

"How are we all going to get home?" cried Mrs. Pinkerton.

Everybody crowded around the doors and tried to help push. But the doors still only opened a little way, and there wasn't room for even the smallest person to squeeze through.

Some of the younger children began to cry. Emma knew that they must be wondering how they would get home to hang up their stockings for Santa.

"Shhh!" said Mrs. Jones, trying to comfort them. "They'll dig us out soon, you'll see."

Suddenly, Sheltie charged toward the crowd of people.

"Sheltie, come back!" cried Emma in

alarm. She raced to grab hold of his bridle, but Sheltie was already in the middle of the crowd.

"Hey, stop that!" shouted Mr. Crock. "You nearly stepped on my toes!"

Lots of other people shouted, too, but Sheltie didn't stop. He kept on barging his way through the crowd until he had reached Dad. And he didn't even stop there. He went on, right to the hall doors.

Emma realized what Sheltie was doing and grinned.

"Don't worry," she said to the villagers. "Sheltie's going to push his way out!"

"Don't be silly!" said Mrs. Pinkerton. "He's only a tiny pony. He can't possibly do anything."

"He may be little, but he's very strong,"

said Emma. "If anyone can do it, he will."
Don't let me down now, boy! she thought,
willing Sheltie to push open the hall doors.

Sheltie stopped in front of the doors as if
considering what to do next. The fierce
wind whistled in and blew the pony's

shaggy hair right over his ears. Icy snow sprayed in, too. Dad jumped back so that he didn't get covered in it.

The little pony pawed at the doors, his hooves slipping on the shiny paint. Then he pushed his body against the doors, but he still couldn't open them.

"There you are, I told you," said Mrs. Pinkerton.

Sheltie moved back a little bit and Charlie dodged out of the way of his back hooves. "Good try, boy," he said. "Come on, guys, let's try again."

But Sheltie wasn't finished yet. He moved back another step, then charged forward with all his might.

"Go, Sheltie, go!" whispered Emma. "You can do it, I know you can!"

The pony's powerful shoulders

pressed against the doors and forced them to open just a little bit more. There was enough room for Sheltie to push his way out now. This meant that there would also be room for people to get out of the hall . . . but they wouldn't be able to go very far. There was still a great wall of snow ahead.

"Oh, clever Sheltie! I knew you could do it," praised Emma. "Well done, boy!"

She waited anxiously to see what the pony would do next. All the villagers watched and waited, too. Sheltie plowed steadily through the wall of snow with his strong little legs. Emma felt so proud of him.

Very soon Sheltie had trampled down enough snow for people to escape. He had

walked right through the snowdrift and
cleared a narrow path.

"Three cheers for Sheltie!" yelled
Charlie. "Now we can all go home and
wait for Santa!"

The villagers cheered and whistled.

"Three cheers for Sheltie! Merry Christmas, everyone!"

Once everyone had gotten past the drifts piled up against the village hall, the snow wasn't so bad. But all the people who had come by car had to leave their cars behind and walk home. Rosie begged to ride home on Sheltie. Emma saddled Sheltie up again and Mr. Crock lifted his granddaughter onto the brave pony. Emma led the two of them back through the village with Mom, Dad, and Joshua following behind.

It had stopped snowing now, and everything was white. Emma thought the houses looked just like frosted cakes. Snow squeaked gently under Sheltie's hooves, but Emma couldn't hear anyone else's footsteps at all.

As they turned into the road, Emma said, "Look, everyone — there's a star."

In the night sky, there was a single bright star.

"Let's all make a wish," said Mom.

The little procession stopped and everyone looked up at the magical star. Emma closed her eyes. What should she wish for? There were so many things! New stirrup leathers for Sheltie?

The old ones were getting very worn. A year's supply of pony-nuts? Or to have lots more fun and adventures with Sheltie next year? It was just too difficult.

She opened her eyes and looked at Rosie on Sheltie's back. The little girl's eyes were shut tight. Emma knew exactly what she was wishing for. She wanted her dad to be home in time for Christmas.

Now Emma knew what her own wish was going to be. She shut her eyes and wished for exactly the same thing as Rosie.

Then Rosie opened her eyes and gave Emma a huge grin.

Somehow Emma was certain that their wish was going to come true.

Wish Come True

Chapter One

Emma woke up to brilliant sunshine.

"Oh, no!" she cried. "I must have overslept!"

And then she remembered.

It was Christmas Day! And it was so bright because of the snow, which had arrived just in time to make it a white Christmas.

Emma found a full stocking at the bottom of her bed. She couldn't hear a sound from the rest of the house. Not even from Joshua's room. How could everyone still be asleep on such a special day? But she knew she could rely on someone to be awake and waiting for her, whatever the time or weather.

Emma pulled back the curtains. Sure

enough, there was Sheltie at the paddock gate, his breath puffing out in clouds in the frosty air.

The little pony was covered with snow. He looked like a snow pony. But Sheltie never felt the cold. His thick, shaggy coat was made for weather like this. And after shoving his way through the snowdrift last night, it was easy for him to trample through the snow from his field shelter to the gate.

"Merry Christmas, Sheltie," Emma whispered. "Since you're the only one up, you can have your Christmas present first!"

Emma dressed quickly in her warmest clothes and tiptoed downstairs to the back door. Sheltie's stocking was waiting by her boots and quilted jacket. It was just as full as her own. Inside there was a new halter and a mixture of carrots, apples, and peppermint treats.

"Sheltie, you're going to love your presents," said Emma softly as she pulled on her boots. She opened the back door and stumbled through the deep snow to the paddock gate. Sheltie blew an excited whinny as soon as he saw her.

Emma climbed over the gate, brushing the snow off the top. Then she draped Sheltie's stocking carefully over the fence.

"Isn't this lovely?" she said, flinging her arms around her snowy pony's neck. "Just wait and see what I've got for you. But first you need a real breakfast."

Sheltie loved the wintry weather. He shook his mane hard so that soft lumps of snow flew into Emma's face.

"Ouch!" said Emma as the freezing stuff hit her. "So you want a game, do you?" She bent to scoop up a ball of snow in each hand and threw them at Sheltie's broad back. Sheltie shied away, dodging the snowballs and whinnying with delight. The pony was just too quick for Emma.

"Got you!" She laughed as one of her snowballs finally caught Sheltie on the rump.

They played for a little longer until Emma said, "That's four for me, and probably about a million for you. Breakfast time!"

Sheltie seemed to know what that

meant. He quickly followed the trail of hoof prints back to his shelter. Emma ran after him.

"There — one scoop and a little extra for luck," she told Sheltie as she emptied the pony-nuts into his feeding manger. Sheltie plunged his head down and munched through it all in seconds.

The water trough had a thick layer of ice on it. Emma bashed at the ice with

a trowel so that Sheltie could get at
the water.

"You'd better have a long drink now,
before it ices over again," she told him.

Emma looked back at her house. All
the curtains were closed, except for hers.
"Everyone's still asleep, Sheltie," she
said as the little pony drank greedily
from his trough. "How can they sleep
in on Christmas Day? I wonder if we're
the only people in the world awake
and ready to open our presents — oh, I
nearly forgot . . ." Emma raced back to
the gate to get Sheltie's stocking. The
Shetland pony looked at his stocking
with great interest and tried to bite it.
Then he nuzzled it. He could obviously
smell the peppermints!

"Since it's Christmas, you can have a

treat for breakfast," said Emma, fishing
out the mints from the top of his
stocking. She took a shiny apple out of
the stocking as well, and put it into her
pocket to give to him later. Then she put on
his new halter.

"Do you think Rosie's dad arrived last
night?" she asked Sheltie.

The pony blew a long, wet raspberry
and dribbled peppermint juice onto
her hand.

Emma decided she and Sheltie
might as well go and see if Rosie's dad
was back. If he wasn't there, at least
they could give Rosie her present to cheer
her up.

Emma went back inside the house to grab
Rosie's present and to check that nobody

was awake yet. Then she led Sheltie up the
road in his new halter.

As they approached Mr. Crock's
house, Emma saw smoke rising from
Mr. Crock's chimney. At least *someone*
was up.

Mr. Crock opened the door to Emma and shook his head sadly.

Oh, dear, thought Emma. *Rosie's dad isn't back yet.*

Rosie peeked out from behind her granddad and waved at Sheltie.

"Merry Christmas, Rosie," said Emma, and handed her a brightly wrapped present.

Rosie loved her toy Shetland pony and decided to call it Sheltie. She smiled bravely, but her eyes were sad.

Suddenly, Mr. Crock's phone rang in the hall. Rosie rushed to stand by her granddad as he answered it.

"It's Daddy for you!" said Mr. Crock, handing Rosie the phone with a grin.

Emma watched anxiously as Rosie

spoke to her dad. Finally, the little girl
put the phone down and gave Emma
a huge grin. Her dad was on his way,
and should be home in time for
Christmas dinner!

Chapter Two

"They're awake at last, Sheltie!" cried
Emma as she arrived home and saw that
all the curtains were open. She flung her
arms around the little pony's neck in
excitement.

Sheltie stomped in the snow and blew
down his nose. His breath puffed out like a
cloud in the frosty air.

"After we've opened our presents, I'll
come out to see you again," Emma

promised. She undid the bolt of the gate and let Sheltie back into his paddock. She quickly took off his new halter, dashed back to the house, and pulled off her snowy boots.

"Merry Christmas, everybody!" said Emma as she burst in through the back door.

Mom, Dad, Emma, and Joshua opened their presents together. It was very exciting, and Emma was delighted with all her new things. She played with Joshua all morning.

After eating a delicious Christmas dinner, Emma decided to go give Sheltie another of his Christmas treats. Sheltie munched on his apple happily and then pushed at the gate. He seemed eager to go for another ride.

"The snow's a bit deep. I don't think Mom and Dad will let us go out on the meadows in case we fall into a snowdrift," said Emma. "But I don't think they'll mind if we go check again to see whether Rosie's dad arrived."

Emma dashed back inside to tell Mom and Dad where she was going, then tacked up Sheltie as fast as she could in the freezing cold. Her fingers were stiff, so it was difficult to do up the buckles. Then she undid the bolt, opened the gate, and let Sheltie through.

The little pony trotted down the road. Emma found it a little tricky riding him through the slippery snow.

"Whoa, Sheltie!" She gasped. "Slow down! We're not in a race!"

But Sheltie seemed to think he was.

He didn't slow down until they reached Mr. Crock's house. He nosed impatiently at the gate. Emma let the little pony through as quickly as she could. As she was closing the gate behind them, Sheltie trotted up the path and took the door knocker in his teeth.

Almost immediately, Rosie opened the door. She was in tears. Her dad still hadn't arrived.

She came out to stroke Sheltie. The Shetland pony seemed to sense that she was upset. He gave soft little whickers and snorts, and rubbed his fuzzy nose into Rosie's hair.

"I'm sure he'll be here very soon," said Emma. "I'll tell you what — would you like Sheltie to take you for a Christmas ride? Mom and Dad won't mind if we just go

down the street. I'll ride home and check
with them."

Rosie grinned. It was the next best thing
to having her dad back!

Emma urged Sheltie to trot home. Mom
and Dad agreed that a little ride on Sheltie
might take Rosie's mind off her dad.

"Poor Rosie," said Mom. "She must be very disappointed. What a good thing she's fallen in love with Sheltie! Here — don't forget to take Joshua's riding helmet with you."

Emma grabbed the riding helmet and ran back out to Sheltie. Together they crunched through the snow, back up the road.

But when they arrived at the house Rosie wasn't ready to go. The little girl had had some bad news. Mr. Crock told Emma what had happened.

"Rosie's dad just called us on his cell phone," said Mr. Crock. He looked anxious. "He got very near Little Applewood, and then his car skidded into a snowdrift. Since he was so close, he decided to abandon it and try to walk here. But everything looks so different in the snow, and now he doesn't know where he is or which way to go. He's completely lost!"

Chapter Three

"What should we do?" Emma gasped. "Should I ask Dad to get the car out?"

"I don't think he'll be able to drive it through the snow," said Mr. Crock. "I think we'll just have to get our boots on and walk! I've called Officer Green. He's out on a job at the moment, but he'll come help as soon as he can."

"I'll go get Mom and Dad. I'm sure they'll want to help, too," said Emma.

Sheltie neighed as she pulled him around and urged him on with her heels. But he seemed to know that Emma was in a hurry. He trotted as quickly and carefully as he could over the snowy ground.

Before Emma had gone very far, she heard a car driving up the road toward her. She brought Sheltie to a stop to let it pass.

"Oh, dear, hurry up," said Emma to herself. "We need to move fast before Rosie's dad freezes in the snow."

But it was Mr. Brown, the farmer, in his truck. As soon as she saw him, Emma realized that he might be able to help. His truck moved easily over the snow. It was made for difficult roads.

Maybe the farmer could help them search for Rosie's dad.

Emma waved frantically at Mr. Brown.

The farmer stopped his truck and rolled down his window. "Is something wrong?" he said.

Emma quickly explained about Rosie's dad, and Mr. Brown agreed to help search for him in the truck.

"You and Sheltie can trot along

beside the truck and help. Sheltie can investigate the snowdrifts," he said. "Ponies have good noses."

"I hope Rosie's dad isn't stuck in a drift!" said Emma anxiously.

"Don't worry," said Mr. Brown. "If he is, at least he'll be out of this cold wind!"

A few minutes later, Emma burst into the kitchen, pink-cheeked and panting.

Sheltie clattered in after her, leaving snowy hoof prints on the tiles. For once, Mom and Dad didn't mind, because they could see how upset Emma was.

"He's lost in the snow!" Emma gasped. "But Mr. Brown will help!"

"Just a minute, Emma," said Mom. "I know you're in hurry, but sit down for a minute and tell us all about it calmly."

Sheltie whickered quietly and pushed
his nose into Emma's hair, as if he agreed
with Mom.

Emma gulped and started again,
explaining about Mr. Crock's phone
call and how she had met Mr. Brown in
the road.

"So Mr. Brown's going to pick up Rosie

and Mr. Crock and we'll all go look for her dad," Emma finished in a rush. "If that's all right," she added.

"That seems very sensible," said Dad. "I've got another idea. Why don't I go to Mr. Crock's house and stay by the telephone? If Rosie's dad phones again, I can give him Mr. Brown's cell phone number. He might be able to describe something near him that one of you recognizes."

"You mean, like the shape of a hill or a clump of trees?" asked Emma.

"Exactly!" said Dad.

Emma tried hard not to be impatient while Dad put on his thick sweater and boots. She led Sheltie outside and sat in his saddle so that they could go as soon as Dad was ready.

Mr. Crock was looking even more anxious when they arrived. Emma soon found out why.

"I just tried Rosie's dad's cell phone number, but there's no answer," he said.

"Never mind," said Dad cheerfully. "I'll stay by the phone and let you know in case he does try to get in touch again. I'll also be able to give Mr. Brown's number to Officer Green when he calls. Then he can get in touch, too, and come help you right away."

Rosie looked sad and frightened as Mr. Brown helped her into the truck.

"Cheer up," said Mr. Crock gruffly as he climbed in after her. "We'll find him, don't worry."

"Sheltie will find him," promised Emma, giving Rosie a quick hug through the open

door of the truck. Then she climbed back onto Sheltie's saddle and waited for Mr. Brown to decide which way to go.

"OK, Emma, this way first, I think," said Mr. Brown, pointing toward the road that led to Fox Hall Manor, where Emma's best friend, Sally, lived. "He'll have turned off the highway and driven toward Beacon Hill and Little Applewood, over the meadows."

Mr. Crock agreed.

Sheltie seemed to take his job very seriously. As they plodded along by the side of the truck, he pushed his sensitive nose into every snowdrift that they passed.

"Good boy, Sheltie," whispered Emma. "If anyone can find him, you can." She pulled the reins gently to show him a new snowdrift, but Sheltie had already seen it and was crossing the road to investigate. He looked so funny with his fat tummy brushing against the deep snow! Emma saw Rosie smiling inside the truck and was glad that Sheltie was keeping the little girl happy.

The truck's engine sounded very noisy in the still air. The road was empty. The fields were empty. Even the woods looked as though no one had entered them for years.

Then suddenly, when they were halfway to Barrow Hill, Emma yelled out, "There's a car!" She could just see the back end of it sticking out into the road at the bottom of the dip.

She urged Sheltie forward. The little pony shook his mane, and his bridle jingled. He snorted loudly, and Emma felt the icy wind rush past her face as Sheltie lifted his hooves high above the thick snow to trot toward the car.

The car was half buried in a snowdrift with its hood in the hedge — just as Rosie's dad had described. But Rosie's

dad had left the car to walk the rest of the way to Little Applewood. He could be anywhere by now!

"This is no weather to be out in," said Mr. Brown quietly to Emma. "I hope we find him soon."

"I'm sure we will," said Emma confidently. But she didn't feel at all sure. She could see Rosie's face through the truck window, looking anxious again. Emma knew that if Rosie's dad had walked toward Little Applewood they would have passed him by now.

"He must have gone the wrong way, back toward the meadows," said Mr. Crock. "Let's move on."

Emma clicked her tongue to tell Sheltie to move on, but the little pony shook his head sideways and tugged at his reins. They were next to an opening in the hedge. It led to a bridle path, then through to open meadows. It was one of Sheltie's favorite rides.

"No, Sheltie," said Emma firmly. "We've got a job to do. We need to stay together if we're going to find Rosie's dad. He wouldn't have gone that way."

But Sheltie whinnied loudly and stomped with his hooves so that snow flew up into his shaggy coat. He pulled hard at his reins, and Emma found it difficult to hold him. She was red in the face from trying to stop him from moving toward the bridle path when Mr. Brown put his head out of the truck.

"Are you OK?" he asked.

"Yes —" began Emma. Then she stopped. "Sheltie seems to want to go this way, over the fields. Maybe he knows something we don't," she said excitedly.

"Are there any footprints?" asked Mr. Brown.

But the wind had blown snow over any footprints that might have been there.

"It's all right," said Emma. "I know the shape of the hills. I won't get lost. And Sheltie can find his way back from anywhere!"

Mr. Crock nodded from inside the car. "Emma's sensible," he muttered. Then he said aloud, "Go on, see what Sheltie can do."

The Shetland pony didn't need any encouragement from Emma. He was off with a spray of snow from his hind legs.

Sheltie seemed to know exactly where he was going, so Emma let him have his way. If she hadn't been so worried, she would have enjoyed the exciting gallop over the fields in the deep snow.

Emma kept looking over at the hedges, just in case Rosie's dad was there, but there was no sign of anyone moving around.

Suddenly, Sheltie slowed to a stop.

"Have you found something, boy?" asked Emma quietly. She held the reins loosely in her lap so that Sheltie could go where he wanted.

The pony's ears pricked up, and he lifted his head to sniff at the frosty air. Then he let out his breath in a puff of white and began to move forward purposefully, heading for the edge of the field. Emma could see huge heaps of snow piled up against the hedge there.

"Whoa, Sheltie! Let me listen," said Emma. "I thought I heard something."

Sheltie stood very still. There wasn't the tiniest jingle from his harness.

Emma heard the noise better this time. It was a voice. Someone was calling.

Chapter Four

"Come on, boy," said Emma excitedly. "Let's go see."

Sheltie galloped across the white field as fast as he could, leaving a trail of hoof prints behind him. As soon as they reached the snowbank, Emma dismounted. "Hello?" she called. "Is anyone there?"

"Th-thank goodness," said a shaking voice.

Emma and Sheltie walked over to where the voice was coming from.

"Are you Rosie's dad?" she called.

"Yes! I'm so glad someone's come," continued the man. "I thought I was going to freeze to death. I piled snow around me to keep warm, but it's not *that* warm!"

Rosie's dad had built a wall of snow around him. Emma peered into the top. He was crouching in his little igloo. He had blue eyes and brown curly hair, just like Rosie.

"We've been looking everywhere for you," said Emma. "You must have gone the wrong way."

"Yes," said Rosie's dad. "I'm obviously not very good at finding my way in the snow — or at building igloos! But who are you, and how do you know about Rosie? Is she all right?"

"I live near Mr. Crock," explained Emma. "He and Rosie are looking for you, too, with Mr. Brown. He's got a truck. If I can borrow your phone, I can call him and tell him where you are," said Emma.

"The battery ran out soon after I called Mr. Crock," said Rosie's dad. "Can you help me get out of here? I'm so cold I can hardly move, and I think I may have twisted my ankle."

"Sheltie can help," said Emma proudly. And before Rosie's dad could ask who Sheltie was, he saw the little Shetland pony's hairy face peering down at him.

"All right, boy, but be careful," said Emma.

Sheltie pawed at the white wall
with his hooves and broke down the
packed snow so that it fell to the ground
in lumps.

"We're nearly there — you'll soon be
out." She scrabbled at the snow with her
gloved hands, pulling chunks of it away.

Sheltie puffed a breath of hot air
down into the middle of the igloo, and
Rosie's dad laughed. "Well done, Sheltie.

That's just what I need to defrost my eyebrows!"

Emma was getting anxious. How would Rosie's dad manage to walk through the snow with a twisted ankle?

Suddenly, Sheltie stopped, pricked up his ears, and whinnied loudly.

"Come on, Sheltie! We've got to get Rosie's dad out before it's dark, and somehow we've got to get him back to the truck!" said Emma frantically.

But then she heard a call from across the snow-covered meadow. She straightened up, feeling almost as stiff as Rosie's dad.

It was Mr. Brown, with Rosie on his shoulders, striding over the field. Close behind came Officer Green.

"He's over here!" cried Emma, feeling

relieved. "But he's hurt his ankle." Sheltie
gave another noisy whinny of welcome
and Rosie's dad let out a faint cheer.

"Daddy, Daddy!" shouted Rosie
excitedly.

Mr. Brown let Rosie down gently in the
snow, and he and Officer Green hurried
over to help her dad.

"It's Daddy dressed as Santa!" said
Rosie.

As the two men pulled Rosie's dad
out of the snow, they all saw what he
was wearing. A bright red coat with
white trim.

He had been all dressed up as Santa
Claus to surprise Rosie when he arrived on
Christmas Day!

Rosie's dad tried to move, but his
ankle was too painful to walk on across the

snowy field back to the truck where
Mr. Crock was waiting for them.

Emma and Rosie had an idea at exactly
the same time.

"He can ride Sheltie!" they said together.

Mr. Brown and Officer Green helped
Rosie's dad onto Sheltie's back, and tucked
Rosie in front of him, wrapped up in the

red coat. Rosie's dad looked very funny
with his long legs dangling down from
Sheltie's broad back! His feet slid gently
along the ground over the snow.

Sheltie went slowly and carefully
across the field. Emma was so proud
of her pony. He might be small, but
Sheltie was the best rescue pony in the
whole world!

Home at last, Rosie's dad thawed out in
front of Mr. Crock's roaring log fire and
rested his leg.

"That's the smartest Shetland pony
I've ever seen," said Rosie's dad as
he told Emma's dad how he had been
found.

Emma beamed with pride. Of course, *she*

knew Sheltie was the smartest pony in the whole world, but it was great when other people thought so, too!

Rosie insisted on bringing Sheltie inside to give him his present of peppermints from the Christmas tree.

"Since it's a special occasion," said Mr. Crock, "I think we could let him in."

But impish Sheltie couldn't wait for his present off the Christmas tree. He looked around the room with a mischievous sparkle in his brown eyes. Then he reached out his long neck and snatched the star from the top of the tree!

"He knows he's a star!" said Rosie's dad, laughing.

Rosie and Emma looked at each other and smiled.

"He's the star I wished on," said Rosie softly. "And he made my wish come true!"